Scholastic
Clifford THE BIG RED DOG

CLIFFORD
and the
Big Ice Cream
Mess

ISBN 0-439-38888-0

10 9 8 7 6 5 4   02 03 04 05 06

Printed in the U.S.A.
First printing, March 2002

Clifford THE BIG RED DOG®

CLIFFORD
and the
Big Ice Cream Mess

Adapted by Josephine Page

Illustrated by Carolyn Bracken and Steve Haefele

**Based on the Scholastic book series
"Clifford The Big Red Dog"
by Norman Bridwell**

From the television script "Screaming for Ice Cream"
by Sheryl Scarborough and Kayte Kuche

Cartwheel
·B·O·O·K·S·®

SCHOLASTIC INC.

New York   Toronto   London   Auckland   Sydney   Mexico City
New Delhi   Hong Kong   Buenos Aires

Hi! I'm Emily Elizabeth, and I have a dog named Clifford. One hot summer day, my friend Charley and I were playing trash-lid hockey.

Clifford played, too! Cleo and T-Bone cheered him on.

Just then, Charley's dad called to us. He owned the Snack Shack. "I'm closing the store for a while," he said. "If you need anything, just go next door to Ms. Kit. She'll help you."

And off he went.

"I'll make you an ice-cream cone," Charley said to me.

I wasn't sure if Charley was allowed to operate the ice cream machine, but it was an awfully hot day, and Charley seemed to know what he was doing.

Just then, a tourist came by. "I'll have an ice-cream cone, too," he said.

"Sure thing," Charley said to the tourist.

"It's okay," Charley said to me. "I help my dad all the time."

It was true that Charley helped his dad while his dad was there. But this was different. And I was beginning to worry.

More tourists came by, all wanting ice-cream cones.

So Charley and I made the cones, Cleo served them, and T-Bone collected the money.

But something went wrong. "I can't stop the machine," Charley said.

All the tourists had gone away by then.

"Eat fast," Charley said. But we couldn't eat fast enough to keep up with the machine. By that time, we were knee-deep in ice cream.

I think T-Bone was frightened. He jumped up on a crate and wouldn't come down.

The machine was making more and more ice
cream. Soon I was up to my waist in the stuff.

I thought Charley should go to Ms. Kit for help.
But Charley wanted to handle things himself.

Meanwhile, the dogs seemed to be having a grand old time. Cleo and T-Bone used trash can lids to surf the ice cream. Clifford blew the ice cream and made big waves for them.

T-Bone seemed to have gotten over
his fear pretty quickly!

But Charley and I weren't having any fun at all.
We were up to our chests in ice cream—and in
deep, deep trouble.

"I wish I knew how to fix this," Charley said.

"I can fix it," said Charley's dad.

He maneuvered the lever, and the machine stopped.

But it was too late. Ice cream was everywhere.

"You should have asked Ms. Kit for help," Charley's dad said.

Charley felt very ashamed. "Sorry, Dad," he said. "I really thought I could handle it."

On that day, Charley and I learned an important lesson—if you need help, ask for it. Charley's dad gave each of us a mop, and together we cleaned that big ice cream mess.

The dogs helped, too. T-Bone and Cleo ate
until they couldn't eat any more.

But Clifford still had room for one last lick!